# At the

written by Rachel Walker
illustrated by Robin Van't Hof

1

We can see
the birds go up.

We can see the birds come down.

We can see the helicopters go up.

We can see
the helicopters
come down.

We can see
the balloons go up.

We can see the
balloons come down.

13

We can see
the planes go up.

15

We can see the parachutes come down, down, down!